Secrets and Surprises

Janey Louise Jones

USBORNE

this time of year, made by Angel Willow in the gown department, from layers of the softest pastel-coloured fleece. Some were edged with feather down, while others were decorated with frosty sparkles, and snowflakes embroidered with satin threads. To go outside, they wore cosy velvet cloaks, with large, feather-trimmed hoods, to keep the winter chill from their ears.

When they were all ready, the girls said goodbye to Sylvie, the dainty pink and silver dove who sat on their windowsill, ready to take messages for the girls whenever they needed her. Gabrielle sometimes worried about Sylvie sitting there all alone, but the pretty bird loved her job as messenger and adored the four Cherubics who she helped look after.

"Have a lovely time," said Sylvie.

"Oh, I wish you could come too," said Gabrielle.

"It's too cold out there for me to leave my perch for long!" said Sylvie. "I'm happy to stay here in the warm."

"I know what," said Gabrielle. "I'll buy some soft wool at the Fair – and I'll knit you a stylish beret and scarf to keep you warm this winter!"

"Oooh, I'd love that," said Sylvie. "I've never had a hat or a scarf before!"

"Good! That's agreed then," said Gabrielle.

"Time to go, everyone!" said Charity.

"Bye for now, Sylvie!" called Gabrielle, as she and the others left their cosy dorm.

"Come on. Let's hurry!" said Hope, as

the four friends floated along the corridors and out into the snowy landscape. "We don't want to miss anything!"

Gabrielle felt a tingle inside. "Wintervale Fair, here we come!" she cried. "I can't wait!"

Chapter 2

When Gabrielle had arrived at Angel
Academy, the first thing she'd noticed was
that all the angels had wings. She'd worried
that without wings she would never fit in
with the other Cherubics – the trainee
Guardian Angels at the school. Luckily the
Head Angel, Madame Seraph, had wished
wings on her at the beginning of term, so
now she looked like a real angel too. As she

flew to the Wintervale Fair, Gabrielle
felt like she'd been flying her
whole life. Below her, Bliss
looked gorgeous with its
wedding-cake houses made
of polished stone, and snow-capped trees.

The four friends flew down into the
town, where, linking arms and floating just
above the ground, they were quickly swept
along in the bustling crowd. There were so
many angels it seemed like everyone on
Cloud Nimbus was making their way to the
Fair this afternoon.

"What sorts of things can we buy at the
Fair?" Gabrielle asked her friends.

"Chocolate, chocolate…and, oh, did I
mention…chocolate?" Ruth giggled.

"The chocolate shop is always there.

It's the most famous thing about Bliss!" said Charity, with a smile. "But there are loads of other things you can buy today. There are stalls selling moonstones, feathers, buttons and bows. There are pretty purses and embroidered shoulder bags, lavender bags and snowdrop posies, antique books, paintings…and then there are lots of other things to do besides shopping."

"Yes," agreed Hope. "I love the games. Last year I threw a hoop over a potion bottle and won a prize. You can play 'Secrets' as well – it's brilliant!"

"What's 'Secrets'?" asked Gabrielle curiously.

"Well," said Hope, "you have to dip your hand into a wooden box and guess what's inside it – and if you guess right, then you win whatever's in there!"

"Oh, I'm definitely going to have a go at that!" said Gabrielle excitedly.

"And of course," said Ruth, "you can have a ride on the famous Crescent-moon Carousel! The seats are all made to look like sparkly moons!"

"That sounds wonderful!" said Gabrielle. "I love carousel rides."

The four angels' cheeks and noses turned pink from the wintery nip in the air as they glided towards the Fair. In the distance Gabrielle heard the beautiful tinkling of bells. Then, as they drew nearer, she noticed the smell of spiced apples and warm toffee. The scene ahead of her looked like an old-fashioned fairground, with stalls, games, and hand-painted merry-go-rounds, but it seemed bathed in a layer of chiffon angel light. The large Crescent-moon Carousel was the centrepiece, and it looked breathtaking, as each crescent seat spun around, sparkling and golden.

"You're going to love this, Gabrielle!" said Ruth, as the four friends landed in one of the bustling streets.

"I know I will," said Gabrielle. "But where shall we start?"

"Let's browse around and see what looks good," suggested Ruth.

There were many wooden stalls in the fairground, all lit with lanterns or candles, and protected with pretty striped canvas shelters. Strings of white roses and silver feathers joined one stall to the next, and hung across the pathways too. Gabrielle thought the Wintervale Fair was even more lovely than she'd imagined and she had to pinch herself to check she wasn't dreaming. She felt like the luckiest girl in the world.

Gabrielle and Hope especially loved all the pretty gifts and crafts on sale at the Fair, but after they'd wandered around for a while, Charity was keen to look for some second-hand textbooks.

"There are always some bargains on the bookstalls, and I'm hoping to buy the first volume of *Vanishing for Angels*, so I can be one step ahead of next week's lesson in the vanishing lab," said Charity.

"Boring!" said Ruth. "I'm not even thinking about schoolwork today! Anyway, we don't have to take the Vanishing Charm until next term."

"Well, I'd like to be prepared," said Charity. "Come on, Hope."

"Erm, do you mind if I go with the others?" mumbled Hope, with blush-pink cheeks. "I quite like looking at the crafts and gifts too."

"Oh, well, okay. It's up to you," said Charity, sounding a little hurt. "See you all later! Let's meet in Coco Lane at Sun Dip."

In the angelic world, everyone used the position of the sun in relation to the big mountain outside Bliss to tell the time. Gabrielle was still trying to get used to it. If they met at Sun Dip today they would be able to get back to Angel Academy in plenty of time for tea.

"Bye, Charity! See you at Sun Dip!" called Gabrielle, as she watched her serious-

minded room-mate head off in the
direction of the bookstalls.

The three girls chatted happily as they
glided along from one pretty craft stall to
the next.

"Now that Charity's gone, I've got
something I can tell you," said Hope.

"What?" asked Ruth.

"I heard a secret earlier on, but Charity
said I had better not repeat it, in case it's
not true," whispered Hope.

"Oh, spill it, please. You've got to now!"
said Ruth.

"Well, you mustn't tell Charity that I
told you!" said Hope.

"Promise!" chimed Ruth and Gabrielle
gleefully.

"All right then… I overheard a

conversation between Angel Fleur and Madame Seraph, while I was helping to decorate the hallway with berries yesterday," said Hope.

Gabrielle and Ruth huddled up to Hope and listened intently. Gabrielle loved secrets and she also loved Angel Fleur, who was her favourite teacher at the Academy.

"They were talking about the end-of-term Charm-giving Ceremony, and you'll never guess what… They think the Snow Angel might be coming to give out the charms!" blurted Hope. "But they're keeping it secret until they know for definite that she's coming."

"Wow!" gasped Ruth, who was generally hard to impress. "That's brilliant. The Snow Angel is a legend! I'd love it if she did come. It would be awesome to meet her."

"Who is the Snow Angel?" asked Gabrielle, suddenly feeling a little left out. "I've never even heard of her before. There are so many things here I still know nothing about."

"Oh, she's so lovely," said Hope. "She lives in the mountain at the top of Cloud Nimbus and she brings winter to the angel world…"

"And she makes raindrops turn into snowflakes, covering the land in the purest white snow…" added Ruth.

"She wears an amazing white cloak which glistens with silver, and she has huge, shimmering wings!" said Hope.

"Oh, and her halo is made from ice crystals," put in Ruth breathlessly. "She visits a different place on Cloud Nimbus each winter. Every town wants her to come – she makes Wintervale!"

"Ooooh, I'd love to see her!" said Gabrielle. "She sounds amazing. I hope she does come. And I hope I'm good enough to get my very first charm."

Gabrielle suddenly felt worried. The Cherubics were each given a charm bracelet on their first day at the Academy. In order to become a Guardian Angel, they had to earn charms and every charm was achieved by mastering a particular angel skill.

First came the Chevalange Charm. Gabrielle and the other Cherubics had

Chapter 3

While Gabrielle was deep in thought,
worrying about the Chevallet routine, she
didn't at first notice that Ruth and Hope
were busy saying hello to many of the
angels they passed. This was Gabrielle's first
ever time at the Fair, but Ruth and Hope
had been many times before. Having been
brought up in the town of Bliss, it seemed
to Gabrielle that her friends knew everyone.

"Oh, look!" said Ruth. "There's Merry Harper, all on her own! Let's see if she wants to join us."

Merry Harper was one angel Gabrielle did recognize. She was a Cherubic from Angel Academy too. Ruth and Merry had been friends at the Petite Angel school, which they'd both attended before joining the Academy. But when Ruth called to her old friend, Merry didn't seem to hear. Instead, she looked over her shoulder anxiously and headed off in the opposite direction. She appeared to be clutching a heavy sack under her velvet cloak and she looked very awkward and nervous.

"Oh, she mustn't have heard me," said Ruth.

Gabrielle thought that seemed odd. It

was almost as if Merry had ignored Ruth, but she'd always been very friendly at the Academy before. She'd even come to Gabrielle's rescue in her first week at the school when she'd had a spot of bother in the Ambroserie refectory.

"I'm sure she did hear," said Hope. "It looked to me as if she was in a hurry."

"Yes," agreed Gabrielle, following Merry's path with her eye. "And it looked like she was hiding something under her cloak, didn't it? I wonder what it could be."

"You're right," said Ruth. "She did look a little secretive just now."

"Maybe she's bought a special Wintervale gift for someone and she wants to keep it secret?" said Gabrielle. "Oh, and that reminds me, I must get some wool for

Sylvie, and some presents for Mum and Dad too! I really want to take them something that has the magical feel of Cloud Nimbus."

"Okay, but let's have some fun first!" said Ruth.

"Brilliant plan!" said Gabrielle. "How about a ride on the carousel. Will you both come with me?"

"Oh yes, of course. Let's do that now!" said Ruth.

"Yippee!" said Hope, joining hands with Gabrielle. "I love the carousel but Charity never wants to go on it. She says it makes her feel dizzy!"

"I want to get as dizzy as I can!" laughed Gabrielle, her heart fluttering with excitement at the thought of it.

Gabrielle and the others arrived at the Crescent-moon Carousel as it was coming to the end of one cycle. It drew to a halt and they each ran to a golden crescent-moon seat. Gabrielle chose a beautiful one, which sparkled prettily in the afternoon light. No sooner were they settled, than the ride began to spin.

"Wow! It's so fast!" called Gabrielle, as it gathered speed.

"It's barely started yet!" shouted Ruth. "Just wait!"

"Oh no! You mean it gets faster?" Gabrielle held on tight.

The carousel gradually built up speed, turning round and round, while the moons went up and down at the same time. No wonder Charity said it made her dizzy.

Gabrielle loved it. She laughed when she got off, and found that she was too wobbly to float in a straight line.

"That was brilliant," she smiled, checking her halo was still in place.

"Oh, it was!" agreed Hope. "I loved it."

"I enjoyed it too," said Ruth, sounding a little disappointed. "But I'd have liked it to go a bit faster!"

Once they'd stopped feeling dizzy, the three friends giggled their way around the Fair, buying little gifts as they went. Purses, pearly hair combs and sparkling baubles all caught Gabrielle's eye, and she managed to get some wool for Sylvie's hat and scarf as well. But every time that Gabrielle and Hope stood mesmerized by pretty crafts and trinkets, Ruth urged them along, and

Gabrielle never managed to find the special gift she wanted for Mum and Dad.

"Come on, you two!" Ruth cried, as Gabrielle and Hope dawdled behind her. "We've seen enough itty-bitty little things now. Look – here's the Secrets stall!"

Gabrielle and Hope linked arms and flew to catch up with her.

The Secrets stall looked intriguing, its closed wooden boxes painted with beautiful abstract designs. Gabrielle examined them on all sides, but there was no telling what was inside. Ruth and Hope urged her to go first so, nervously, Gabrielle placed her hand inside one of the wooden boxes. "Aarggh!" she cried. "This is a bit scary!"

After a moment clutching at thin air, her fingers touched the mystery object. It was cold. Smooth.

"It actually feels lovely!" she said finally, with relief.

What could it be? It made her think of the texture of the gemstones on one of the summer dresses she'd been given when she'd first arrived at the Academy.

"Is it a moonstone?" she asked.

The angel in charge of the game opened the box slowly…

"Ta-da!" Ruth laughed, enjoying the tension.

Gabrielle was right! "Hurray! I love moonstones," she said. "I'll give this to Mum in the Christmas holidays!"

Ruth took a turn next and came away empty-handed, after guessing "sweetie" when in fact what she'd been feeling was a marble! Hope was equally unlucky when what she'd thought was an orange had turned out to be a bouncing ball.

"Come on," said Ruth. "That's enough secrets for now. Time to buy chocolate!"

The girls turned into Coco Lane and saw Merry again up ahead. She was still struggling with the heavy sack and as soon as she saw the other Cherubics, she bolted off in the opposite direction. She even tried to take to the sky, but with whatever she was carrying, flying proved impossible. Gabrielle watched Merry curiously. What was she up to, and why was she avoiding her friends?

Ruth interrupted Gabrielle's

thoughts. "Let's worry about Merry later!" she said. "We're at the chocolate shop now!"

Gabrielle spun around and stared ahead, wide-eyed. In front of her in this little lane, in the middle of the angelic town of Bliss, which was itself in the middle of the angelic world of Cloud Nimbus, stood the most exquisite shop she had ever seen. Gabrielle and her friends stepped into a chocolate wonderland. There were gold cabinets lining the walls, and within the cabinets were chocolate hearts, bars, balls, coins, bunnies, eggs, lollipops, stars and flowers. As Gabrielle looked towards the back of the shop, she saw a little group of angels busily working with liquid chocolate.

Some poured the dark fluid into
moulds, while others packaged
firm-set chocolate into golden
boxes, tied with
 brightly coloured ribbons.
"What did I tell you?" said
Ruth. "This is the place to come!"

"I agree – it's chocolicious," said
Gabrielle, laughing in delight. "What shall
we buy?"

"We can get a Lucky Dip of goodies if
we put our coins together. It will keep us
going for at least a week!" said Ruth.

As they each took a turn pulling a
package out of the Lucky Dip, Gabrielle
turned to Hope.

"This is enough chocolate for a whole
year, never mind one week!" she giggled.

"I'm sure we'll get through it quicker than you think!" smiled Hope, smacking her lips together.

After the chocolate shop, the girls bought some sparkling Wintervale baubles for Crystals in a neighbouring shop, and as the town clock struck Sun Dip, Charity caught up with them.

"Have you all had a good time?" she asked. "I've found a brilliant book on vanishing. I can't wait to get back and read it."

The others all groaned, but Charity had reminded them that Madame would be expecting them back at the Academy soon. The trip to the Wintervale Fair had ended too quickly, as far as Gabrielle was concerned. She still hadn't found a gift for Mum and Dad.

As the four Cherubics flew back to school,

they saw Merry Harper flying towards them, without the heavy sack. This time Merry waved and managed a weak smile.

"Merry looks tired," said Hope. "I wonder what she's done with the sack."

"Who knows?" said Ruth. And they carried on with their excited chatter and quite forgot about Merry for the moment.

Sylvie was delighted when the girls arrived back in their room and she was absolutely thrilled with the pink wool that Gabrielle showed her.

"I'm going to get knitting straight away!" said Gabrielle. "I just hope my knitting's good enough!"

"Thank you so much!" cried Sylvie. "I'm sure you will do a fine job."

The angels settled down for a cosy time in Crystals. Gabrielle sat with her knitting needles clicking as she got on with making Sylvie's matching hat and scarf, while Charity had her head in the vanishing book she had bought, and Ruth and Hope giggled a lot as they stacked the chocolate supplies in various spaces around the room, tasting bits here and there as they went.

"My goodness, what is that young angel doing?" exclaimed Sylvie suddenly, from her spot on the windowsill.

"What's going on?" asked Gabrielle.

"Come and look!" the little bird said.

The four angels peered out of the window and saw Merry flying off again. Her hair was messy under her halo and her cloak hung untidily off one shoulder.

"Why is she flying so awkwardly?" asked Sylvie.

"I don't know," said Ruth. "But she was acting strangely at the Fair too."

"It looks like she's carrying something again," said Gabrielle. "I'd love to find out what she's up to."

Chapter 4

The next day was Sunday, and the four
Cherubics finished their chores early, then
found themselves with some spare time in
the afternoon.

"What shall we do?" said Ruth. "I wish
we could start practising vanishing!"

"There's no way we can do that until
Angel Peter has taught us what to do," said
Charity.

"But you've been swotting up on it," Ruth replied with a grin. "Couldn't you try and teach us?"

The Cherubics had to learn to vanish so that when they went on secret Guardian Angel missions to Earth they wouldn't be spotted. Gabrielle was keen to learn but the idea was a little bit scary. She agreed with Charity that they should wait for Angel Peter, the teacher for the Vanishing Arts, to show them how to do it properly.

"I'd really like to go and help Angel Willow in the gown department," said Gabrielle. "She's got masses of work to do, what with making our tutus for the Chevallet test as well as all the Charm-giving gowns."

Since she'd been at the Academy,

Gabrielle had proved to be very neat in sewing classes, and busy Angel Willow, who made all the angel gowns at the Academy, was delighted when Gabrielle had offered to help out in her spare time. She'd previously been allowed to sew buttons and moonstones on some of the angel gowns, and Angel Willow had even taught her how to embroider dainty flowers onto the delicate fabric.

It made Gabrielle a little homesick, as this was the sort of work she and Mum used to do together in wintertime at home. They would sit by the fire, doing cross-stitch and sewing pretty buttons onto dresses.

"Oh, sewing! Boring!" said Ruth. "If we can't try vanishing, then I'd like to practise some Angelfly moves by the turrets!"

Gabrielle had learned enough Angelfly dance moves to join in a display the Cherubics had put on for Parents' Day, but she didn't fancy practising outside when it was so cold.

"Well, why don't we each do our own thing, and then meet up at teatime?" suggested Gabrielle.

"But aren't best friends supposed to do everything together?" countered Ruth, looking a little gloomy.

"Can't we have our own hobbies and still be best friends?" said Gabrielle.

"I s'pose," said Ruth.

As Gabrielle tidied her hair, Hope said, "Can I come with you, Gabrielle? I love sewing too."

"Of course!" said Gabrielle. "I'm sure Willow needs all the help we can give just now." The two room-mates set off together.

"Bye then," called Ruth, looking a little miserable.

"Bye, Ruth," called Gabrielle over her shoulder. She hoped she hadn't upset her best friend.

When Gabrielle and Hope arrived at the gown department, Angel Willow was sitting in her favourite window seat, with her small gold spectacles on her nose and her wild blonde hair caught back in a band, showing off her lovely high cheekbones. She  was surrounded by half-finished gowns, rolls of gorgeous tulle and silky fabrics, plus threads, buttons and bows.

The open wardrobes revealed rails of floaty angelic gowns, and there were shelves and boxes stacked with every kind of button, ribbon, trim and gemstone imaginable. And as for the angel shoes stacked neatly in rows… Gabrielle longed to try each pair, but she had to remember that there was work to be done.

"Hello, Angel Willow. Are there any jobs we can do for you today?" said Gabrielle. "Hope would like to help out as well."

"Oh, how lovely to have the two of you here. It's such a busy time of year. I've got the tutus to make for the Chevallet routines and gowns for the Charm-giving Ceremony too. There are moonstones waiting to be stitched onto a gown

I worked on earlier," said Willow. "And perhaps you could add a few of the embroidered flowers to this one here, girls? Gabrielle, you made such a lovely job of those before. You could show Hope what to do."

"I'd love to!" said Gabrielle.

"Thanks," said Hope. "I'll be very careful!"

Once they had the gowns and all the threads and dainty accessories they needed, Gabrielle and Hope settled down next to Willow. They worked quietly together, enjoying each other's company.

Gabrielle was engrossed in her work, but after some time, she heard someone approaching outside in the corridor. She'd noticed that with angels you didn't hear footsteps, as their feet rarely touched the ground, but there was a certain familiar swish of wings. She looked up at the doorway as a shadow fell across it.

Gabrielle smiled with surprise. "Hello, Ruth. Have you come to join us?"

"No, not really," said Ruth. "But I'm bored on my own and I just wondered how you and Hope were getting along."

"It's fun!" said Hope. "Gabrielle's a brilliant teacher."

Ruth hung her head.

"Is everything okay?" asked Gabrielle.

"Yeah. It's just that I'm no good at sewing and I have no one to hang out with," she replied sadly. "Charity's got her nose stuck in that vanishing book again."

"Oh, why don't you try and help us here? There are so many jobs to do and we can chat as we work," said Gabrielle.

"Well, if you won't do what I want to do, I suppose I'll have to do what you're doing," said Ruth.

"I know," said Angel Willow, "why don't you try a little tester of stitches first? I have some spare fabric."

Ruth sat between Gabrielle and Hope, took a needle and thread and tried to copy the daisy stitches they were doing.

"It's not that tricky," she decided, as she pierced the needle through the delicate fabric.

"That's really neat stitching," said Gabrielle. "Isn't it fun?"

"I wouldn't go that far, but it's not as boring as I thought," admitted Ruth.

Ruth tried her best and, for a while, she managed to copy Gabrielle, but as she got bored and fidgety, she stabbed the needle through a thicker section of the fabric. "Ouch!" she cried, as she pricked her finger and a spot of blood fell onto the pretty gown that Gabrielle was working on.

"Oh Ruth!" exclaimed Gabrielle. "Look at the mess!"

"What about me? I've hurt myself," complained Ruth.

"I know, I'm sorry it's just that…" But Gabrielle stopped when she saw how upset Ruth was.

Ruth put her needle down, while Angel Willow fetched the first-aid box.

"We'll soon get you patched up, Ruth," said Willow.

"Sorry I'm so clumsy!" said Ruth. "I give up! Obviously you were getting along much better without me."

"Never mind!" said Gabrielle, a little more sharply than she intended.

"But you do mind," said Ruth. "I'm no good at stuff like this."

Ruth got up in a strop and flew out of the gown department, leaving Willow standing helplessly with the first-aid box.

"Oh dear," said Gabrielle. "I think I was a bit mean to Ruth. She was only trying to help. I should go after her."

"Yes," agreed Hope. "She must have felt left out because the two of us came here together…"

"Of course. Yes, you're right," said Gabrielle. "What an idiot I am. I need to say sorry. Poor Ruth! I've been so thoughtless."

"I'll carry on here and you go and find

her," said Hope. "I don't want you two falling out!"

"Thanks, Hope. Is that okay, Angel Willow?" asked Gabrielle.

"Of course. We don't want anyone to feel unwelcome here," replied the teacher. "And it is always lovely to see you girls working as a strong team!"

Gabrielle placed her sewing things neatly to one side and dashed out of the room in search of Ruth. But by the time she got out into the corridor, her friend was nowhere to be seen.

Chapter 5

Gabrielle wondered where Ruth could be. *Maybe she's gone back outside,* she thought. Although she didn't have her cloak, Gabrielle flew out into the garlanded courtyard and saw nobody at first. But then she thought she spotted Ruth hiding behind a pillar. As Gabrielle approached the pillar, she heard a muffled giggle.

"Ruth? Is that you?" called Gabrielle.

There was no reply. *She's hiding from me!* thought Gabrielle.

There was another giggle. *She's definitely here, and she's playing games!*

"Ruth? I'm sorry. I didn't mean to make you feel left out. It was nice of you to try and help with the gowns," said Gabrielle.

As she reached the pillar, she saw Ruth fly off in the opposite direction.

Gabrielle followed her. "Ruth," she called. "Stop and talk to me."

But Ruth was in the mood for some fun. She was a much more experienced flyer than Gabrielle and she began to dart this way and that, swooping over the snowy gardens which surrounded Angel Academy. There was no time to feel cold as Gabrielle chased her friend here and there.

Worn out, Gabrielle stopped to rest on the branch of a tree and peered round to try to see where Ruth had gone. Just then, a snowball whistled past, narrowly missing Gabrielle's ear!

Oh, so she wants a snowball fight! thought Gabrielle.

She scooped some snow from the tree branches, quickly pressing it into a snowball, and when Ruth peeked out from behind a bush, Gabrielle threw it.

Splat! It hit Ruth on the nose!

Oh no! thought Gabrielle. *Now she'll be even madder with me!*

"Whoops! Sorry about that!" she called. "And I'm sorry about just now. I know you hate sewing. It was so nice of you to try!"

Ruth flew up to the tree and perched next to Gabrielle. She smiled sheepishly, and gave her friend a quick hug, but then her eye caught something in the distance. Gabrielle watched as a look of concern spread across Ruth's face.

"Oh, Gabrielle!" she cried. "There's someone slumped in the doorway of that little shed. She's not moving."

"Oh my goodness!" said Gabrielle anxiously. "We must go and help."

Gabrielle and Ruth flew down to where the angel lay.

"It's Merry!" Gabrielle gasped, dizzy with worry.

Merry's violet velvet cloak looked vibrant against the pure white blanket of snow that covered the courtyard, but her face was almost as white as the snow, and her lips were colourless too.

"Merry?" said Ruth softly. "Are you okay?"

Merry moved her head a little at the sound of Ruth's voice.

"Phew. Thank goodness she can hear us," said Ruth.

Gabrielle took Merry's icy hands and rubbed them in her own to warm them up.

"Merry, talk to us. Are you ill?" asked Gabrielle. "What happened? Why are you lying here?"

Merry began to mumble: "So tired. Must help Anoushka…"

Gabrielle looked at Ruth. "Who is Anoushka?" she asked.

Ruth shrugged her shoulders and said, "Merry, who is Anoushka?"

Suddenly Merry sat upright and rubbed her eyes. "Oh dear. What did I say?" she muttered, coming to life.

"Not much," said Ruth. "Just that you were tired, and you mentioned Anoushka."

"Oh, I must have been dreaming. I had to stop here for a little rest and I must have fallen asleep," said Merry.

"Thank goodness you were just sleeping. But you could have been frozen to death, silly billy!" said Ruth. "So, anyway, who is Anoushka?"

Merry looked panic-stricken. "Erm, Anoushka? I don't know," she said nervously.

"Come on, Merry. What's going on?

You'll feel better if you tell us. Maybe we can help," offered Gabrielle sympathetically.

"There's nothing to tell. I'm tired, that's all. It's been a busy term," said Merry. With that, Merry got up and tried to fly back towards the school. But instead she collapsed in a heap in the snow.

"You look exhausted; we'll help you back," said Gabrielle. "Put your arms around us."

"Thank you," said Merry, with a faint smile on her pale lips.

After Gabrielle and Ruth delivered Merry safely to Silverlight, her dormitory, and got her settled into her cosy bed, they went to find Angel Fleur to ask her to keep an eye on their friend. Although Angel Fleur was keen to know what had happened, the two room-mates didn't want to get Merry into trouble. They told Fleur that Merry had been playing in the snow with them and had got too cold. Luckily, their teacher seemed satisfied with that explanation.

With their earlier disagreement completely forgotten now, the girls discussed Merry's strange behaviour on the way back to Crystals.

"What is she up to?" said Ruth.

"I wish I knew. There's definitely something going on," said Gabrielle. And we must try to find out what it is!"

Chapter 6

The first lesson on Monday morning
was at the stables. The Cherubics were
to start work on their Chevallet dance
routines with their chevalanges. For
Gabrielle the combination of horses and
ballet, with angel wings too, couldn't have
been more perfect. However, the
Cherubics had learned that an external
examiner – an angel called Mademoiselle

Balance – would be coming to the
Academy to judge the Chevallet routines
later in the term. The thought made
Gabrielle jittery with nerves, but she
pushed her fears to the back of her mind
and tried to focus on ideas for her routine.

After a delicious hot breakfast in the
Ambroserie, the four girls from Crystals
flew to the stables together, over the lake
and across the rolling grounds of Angel
Academy. By now Gabrielle's head was full
of lovely Chevallet moves, inspired by their
Angelfly teacher, Angel Anna. She couldn't
wait to suggest these to Domino and then
work on them together until their routine
was perfect.

The stable block was made up of a series
of buildings around a courtyard next to the

chevalange paddock. There were many chevalanges to house and each had its own large stable, overlooking the central courtyard, and every four stables had an adjoining tack room.

Gabrielle loved everything about the stables. The chevalanges were all so kind and friendly, and she enjoyed studying the coloured brushes and combs, soaps and potions, as well as the bejewelled bridles and saddles in the tack room that were used for special occasions. Sometimes she would polish the tack, and at other times she would groom Domino, as she had been taught to do.

Having her own angelic horse was one of the most exciting things about being a trainee Guardian Angel. Gabrielle

remembered fondly the day
Domino had come to collect her
from Earth, when she'd first joined the
Academy. He'd proved to be a wise and
helpful partner since then and, during these
sessions, they always chatted easily
to one another. And if Domino
found some of her ideas for decorating
his mane and tail a little girlish, he never
said so.

Gabrielle made a beeline for Domino's
stall. She was buzzing with ideas about
their Chevallet routine and dying to get
started. Now that it was midwinter, her
beautiful grey angel horse spent most of his
time indoors, snuggling into his soft
bedding, protected from the chill wind,
with his vast wings resting across his back.

But today Domino's stable was empty.

Gabrielle had a look around the stable block and went out to the paddock. But there was no sign of Domino anywhere. Ruth and her chevalange, Humphrey, were already practising their Chevallet steps and it looked like they were having lots of fun.

"Hi, you two," called Gabrielle. "Humphrey, have you seen Domino today? I can't find him."

"Yes. He left just before you got here," said Humphrey. "He went away with Posy – Merry's chevalange."

"That's strange," said Gabrielle, puzzled. "Why would Domino and Posy go off together? They knew we were coming to start on our Chevallet routines today."

"I'm not sure," said Humphrey. "One of

the messenger doves came down earlier, spoke to Posy and they left in a bit of a hurry. Domino said to tell you he'd come back as soon as he could."

"Okay," said Gabrielle, feeling more than a little disappointed.

She went back inside and, as she polished up Domino's best saddle in preparation for the Chevallet routine, Hope appeared at the tack-room door with a clipboard and pen in her hands.

"Hi, Gabrielle! I'm doing a job for Angel Raphael. He wants me to make a list of questions about Chevallet for the second part of the lesson." Angel Raphael was the Chevalange Care teacher and in charge of running the stables. "Have you got any questions?" Hope asked.

"Well, apart from 'Where is my chevalange?' I'd like to ask if we have to stay close to our chevalanges during the routine, or if we can fly around the sky away from them," said Gabrielle flatly.

"Okay, I'll make a note of that," said Hope, "though it might be a question for Angel Anna… What do you mean you don't know where Domino is?"

"He went off with Merry's chevalange earlier, but that's all I know," said Gabrielle.

"Hmm, that's very odd." Hope frowned.

"It is," Gabrielle agreed.

"Well, I've got to ask everyone if they have any questions, so I'd better get on with it," said Hope. "But I'll see if anyone knows where he's gone while I'm at it."

"Okay, thanks. See you later," said
Gabrielle.

She decided to cut lengths of ribbon
so that she could braid little sections of
Domino's mane and tie the ends. Just as she
cut the last length from the roll, Hope
reappeared at the door.

"It's me again," said Hope. "Have you
seen Merry this morning?"

"Erm, no, actually," said Gabrielle. "But
she might be sick because, remember, she
fell asleep in the snow yesterday and she
looked really chilled and shivery when Ruth
and I took her back to her dorm. But it's
weird that Posy isn't here either."

"Yes, very peculiar," agreed Hope.

"She's been behaving oddly ever since the
Wintervale Fair, hasn't she?" said Gabrielle.

"Definitely," Hope frowned. "And if she starts missing lessons, she might not get her charm."

Hope and Gabrielle went in search of Merry, looking in every part of the stables.

"There's Fey and Iris and their chevalanges…" said Hope.

"And we know Ruth's in the courtyard," said Gabrielle.

"Yes, and here's Ella, Penny and Frankie…" said Hope.

"Tamsin, Pansy and Feather are in this tack room," said Gabrielle.

"So, everyone's here, but there's definitely no sign of Merry," said Hope. "We'd better go and tell Angel Raphael."

Their teacher was in the courtyard, overseeing some of the Cherubics who were checking their chevalanges' hoofs.

"Excuse me, Angel Raphael," said Hope. "I've collected nearly all the questions, but I can't find Merry."

"Oh, that's odd," said Raphael, with a note of concern in his voice. "Madame Seraph's messenger dove usually lets me know if someone is absent."

"And it's also odd that Domino isn't here," said Gabrielle. "And Posy's missing too."

"Yes, that's very strange…" said Raphael. "Why did no one tell me sooner? I'd better find out what's going on."

A little while later Angel Raphael gathered the Cherubics together in the courtyard. "First of all, I must say I can't understand why Merry and two chevalanges are missing from the lesson this morning. Can anyone shed some light on their disappearance?" The Cherubics all looked around at each other, shrugging and shaking their heads.

"Very well. I have sent a messenger dove to Madame Seraph, but until we have any news let's see," he said, consulting his list. "The first question is 'Are there any special moves you must demonstrate during the Chevallet test?' Hmm. That is more a question for Angel Anna…she looks after the ballet. My job is to make sure that the chevalanges are taken care of and beautifully presented…"

Gabrielle wasn't really listening as Angel Raphael answered their questions. It seemed pointless being at the stables without her lovely Domino.

Chapter 7

Gabrielle and Ruth flew slowly back to the school after the lesson, chatting about ideas for their Chevallet routines. As the two best friends flew along a line of trees near the river, Gabrielle thought she heard a faint cry in the distance.

"What was that?"

"What?" said Ruth.

"It was a cry or whimper, I'm sure of it,"

said Gabrielle. "It was coming from the river. Let's see what's going on."

"Okay," said Ruth. "It's breaktime anyway, so we won't be missed in school for a while."

The two angels swooped over the frosty trees, above a path that led to the banks of the fast-flowing river.

"Help! I can't hold on much longer…" cried a faint voice.

"Oh. I heard that!" said Ruth.

"Look! There's Domino and Posy," cried Gabrielle anxiously.

The two chevalanges were wading along the edge of the water, looking worried. They were both focused on a large rock in front of them. Wedged between the rock and a log in the gushing, icy water was

Merry. Most of her body was submerged and she looked half frozen and very distressed, though she managed a faint smile when she saw her friends flying towards her.

"She must have fallen in," gasped Gabrielle, as she and Ruth flew swiftly towards the rock.

"Can you help me, p-please?" cried Merry.

As Gabrielle and Ruth hovered above Merry, Domino called out to them.

"Girls!" he sighed with relief. "Thank goodness! How did you find us here?"

"We heard a cry," said Gabrielle. "But we've been worried about the three of you all morning."

"Yes, poor Merry got stuck in the river

before class and her messenger dove came
to tell Posy that she was in trouble. I
offered to come along to help. We've been
trying to shift that log but we can't do it on
our own. We need some rope so that I can
pull her free," said Domino.

"We can help," said Gabrielle. "One of
us can fly back to the school to get some
rope."

"I'll go!" said Ruth. "I can fly fastest!"

"Try the sewing department," suggested
Gabrielle. "I know Angel Willow keeps
plenty of strong cord there for our cloaks."

"Thank you, Ruth!" said Domino and
Posy in unison.

"You'd better make our excuses for the
next class," said Gabrielle. "We're definitely
going to be late now."

"Okay, I'll think of something," said Ruth. As she disappeared into the distance, Gabrielle turned to Merry.

"Don't worry. We'll soon get you out of here. But what were you doing?" she asked.

"Erm…I was out getting some f-fresh air before b-breakfast…" Merry began, her teeth chattering.

"But there's a pile of driftwood at the water's edge," said Posy. "Were you collecting wood, Merry?"

"No," said Merry, but her tired face looked guilty.

"The main thing is that we get you free," said Gabrielle, trying to forget about the wood. "It won't be long before Ruth gets back, I promise!"

"Th-thank you, G-Gabrielle!" chittered

Merry. "I-I've n-never been s-so cold."

A few moments later, they heard Ruth's voice in the distance.

"I'm coming!" she called. "I've got some cord! And a cosy blanket too!"

"Hurray!" chorused Gabrielle and the two worried chevalanges.

When Ruth arrived, Gabrielle tied one end of the cord around Domino's strong chest, while Ruth flew over to the log that was jamming Merry to the rock. Hovering precariously, Ruth managed to tie the other end around it.

Posy looked on anxiously.

"Not long now, Merry – you'll be out soon," said Gabrielle, flying to join Ruth above the rock.

"Okay, Domino, ready?" Gabrielle called.

Domino gave a nod then began to pull forwards. At first, the log didn't move, but after another big pull, it shifted a fraction.

"We should be able to lift Merry free now!" said Gabrielle.

The girls each hooked a hand under Merry's arms, and, as they lifted her a little, and Domino pulled on the log once more, Merry began to move with them.

"We've got her!" cried Gabrielle triumphantly.

Merry was limp and exhausted, as well as soaking wet, her clothes and wings heavy with freezing cold water, but they managed to help her fly to the riverbank.

Posy was beside herself with concern for her Cherubic. "Put her on my back and I will take her back to school," she said.

Merry was too tired and chilled to try to use her wings again, so the girls lifted her onto Posy and wrapped the soft blanket around her.

"T-thank you so much," whispered Merry, between huge shudders.

"She must get to bed immediately," said Gabrielle, "with a mug of creamy hot chocolate."

"Oooh, that sounds so nice," said Merry wearily.

"Thank you, girls," said Domino. "We couldn't have done it without you."

"Hear, hear!" agreed Posy. "You have been quite wonderful."

"It was the least we could do," Gabrielle smiled shyly.

"And I'm sorry I missed you at the

stables!" said Domino. "But I promise we'll find some extra time to work on our Chevallet routine soon!"

"Thank you, Domino," said Gabrielle, with a broad smile. "I will sketch out a routine in my notebook and then we can begin to rehearse." But Gabrielle's smile faded as she looked back towards the icy river.

We must get Merry to tell us what she was doing near the river in the first place, she thought. It was the second time they'd had to help Merry out of trouble. Why did she keep going off on strange errands in the freezing weather?

"Come on, girls, let's get you back to the Academy," said Domino. "You all need to get warm and dry."

* * *

The chevalanges landed on the snowy school lawns, where Gabrielle and Ruth helped Merry down from Posy's back.

"We'll see her to her room," said Gabrielle.

"Thank you so much," said Posy. "Rest well, Merry!"

The girls helped Merry up to her dorm and waited while she struggled out of her wet clothes, then they got her settled into bed. Her dorm's messenger dove, who was anxious to know what had been going on, arranged for a hot chocolate to be delivered.

"We'll come and see you later!" said Gabrielle. "I just hope you haven't caught a chill."

"I'm better already!" said Merry. "But please don't say anything to Angel Fleur this time or I'll be in so much trouble!"

"Okay, so long as you don't move a muscle. You need to rest and we'd better get to Art," said Ruth.

The two friends were soaking wet after helping Merry, so they quickly went to change and tidy their hair in Crystals, before heading to their Art class.

"Oh, hello!" said Sylvie from her perch. "What are you two doing here at this time? And why are you all wet?"

"It's a long story," said Gabrielle. "Merry was stuck in the river…"

"Merry? But I've just seen her fly past the window."

"What?" Gabrielle and Ruth exclaimed in unison.

"It was Merry," repeated the little dove. "But she should be in lessons. And so should you. Whatever's going on?"

"We rescued her from the river where she'd fallen in. She was exhausted and freezing so we put her to bed," said Gabrielle, peering out of the window. "Why on earth has she gone out again?"

"Let's go after her!" said Ruth.

"But you must get back to class," said Sylvie anxiously. "You've already missed half of a lesson. You mustn't miss any more."

"You're right, Sylvie," said Gabrielle. "But I'm worried about Merry. She shouldn't be out of bed, let alone out of the Academy."

* * *

After the Art lesson, it was time for lunch.
Gabrielle, Ruth, Charity and Hope chatted
about Merry as they ate.

"I think she's got a secret friend," said
Hope.

"Maybe," said Ruth. "But why would
a friend need lengths of driftwood, and all
that stuff she was carrying at the
Wintervale Fair?"

"Hmm," said Gabrielle. "Whatever she's
up to it seems very important to her. She's
taking a lot of risks…"

"Have you tried asking her?" suggested
Charity logically.

"Yes, but she denies that anything is
wrong," said Ruth.

"She's keeping something secret, for

sure," agreed Hope.

"But she's going to get in trouble soon or put herself in more danger and we just want to help!" said Gabrielle, her voice filled with frustration.

Chapter 8

In between normal lessons, most of the
Cherubics and their chevalanges practised
their Chevallet routines whenever they
could. Angel Anna, the Angelfly teacher
and Angel Raphael were always on hand
to help. Gabrielle and Domino wanted to
make their routine thrillingly different,
whilst making a good job of the
compulsory moves as well.

"What I have in mind," said Gabrielle, as she showed Domino her sketch pad with the moves all numbered in sequence, "is that we should mirror one another by doing the same moves at the same time, and then come back together for a finale. If we fly to the left, then spin for four beats, then twirl for four and leap into a jeté…"

"Sounds good," said Domino. "Why don't you dance it through and I'll watch, then I can join in with you next time round?"

"Great, I'll show you what I mean," said Gabrielle. She hummed the tune she wanted to use for the routine as she took off and swooped gracefully through the air, using her arms and hands to express emotion. As she spun, twirled, leaped and

floated, she forgot all about her worries
and anxieties.

When she flew to the ground, she
noticed that all the Cherubics and
chevalanges had stopped to watch her.
They began to applaud.

"That was a beautiful display!" said Ruth.
"You're a natural!"

"Oh, I didn't mean for everyone to
watch!" Gabrielle said, blushing.

Now Domino flew into the air and
majestically danced the routine through
with Gabrielle, using his vast wingspan to
move with speed and elegance. This time
Gabrielle was a little more self-conscious
and she couldn't help glancing down at
the ground.

Out of the corner of her eye she

noticed Merry was getting on with her routine as best she could, though she still looked pale and weak. During a break, Gabrielle approached her and asked how she was.

"A bit better, but still aching all over," said Merry.

"You must be," said Gabrielle kindly. "Whatever were you doing at the river?" she asked. "Getting trapped like that must have been so scary."

"You're very kind, Gabrielle, and you know I'm beginning to think I can't do this on my own…"

"Come on, Cherubics, there's no time for chit-chat," interrupted Angel Anna, smiling. "You need to concentrate on your routines now."

"Meet me in the gardens after tea tonight," whispered Merry.

"Okay," Gabrielle quickly nodded.

"But please don't tell a soul," added Merry.

"Of course not. I promise," said Gabrielle.

The afternoon couldn't pass fast enough for Gabrielle. She was curious about Merry's secret, but above all, she wanted to help Merry before she got into even more serious trouble.

Even though she was itching to tell Ruth about her plans, she knew she could not break her promise to Merry. So, during tea, she told a little white lie. She felt guilty, but she didn't want to upset her best friend again.

"I'm going to do some sewing after tea," she fibbed, knowing this was something Ruth would not be interested in, especially after the last time.

"Good luck with that," said Ruth. "I can't think of anything worse than stabbing my fingers again. I've got some homework to finish anyway."

Phew, thought Gabrielle.

After tea, Gabrielle brushed her hair, adjusted her halo and prepared to leave the dorm. *Drat*, she thought. *If I take my cloak, the others will know I'm going outside. But if I don't take it, I'll freeze.* Then she had an idea. "Oh, look," she said, picking up her white cloak. "The hem is fraying."

"Why not take it down to the gown department with you?" suggested Ruth.

"Good idea." Gabrielle dreaded Hope saying she'd come too, but Hope didn't mention it. *Perhaps because it upset Ruth so much the last time*, she thought.

Gabrielle straightened her halo and floated down the corridors and out to the garden to meet Merry, stopping briefly by the door to put on her cloak. She kept to the shadows in case Sylvie noticed her out of doors. Sylvie was a kind and understanding dove, but Gabrielle didn't want her asking any awkward questions right now.

Gabrielle wasn't sure where she and Merry were supposed to meet, so she found a spot in the gardens where she could look around, but no one could see her.

Time passed, and there was no sign of

Merry, so Gabrielle began to think she
must have got the details wrong. Surely
Merry should be here by now? She began
to flit around, peeking out from behind
trees and turrets, looking this way and
that. Then she flew around the lake,
but a snowy owl swooping between
the silent tree branches was the only
sign of life she saw.

After that, Gabrielle flew over
the Ambroserie and the school hall,
heading for the front of the school. As
she passed the school kitchens, she looked
down and saw some movement in a bush
below.

She stopped to perch on the high wall
of the kitchen garden. She hadn't seen this
garden before, and even though it was

covered with thick snow, she could still smell delicious herbs in the air.

Gabrielle trained her eyes on the bush once more. It moved again, and now she could see part of an angelic wing peeking out. It had to be Merry. But why was she hiding in a bush? Gabrielle decided to fly down to find out what was going on. But before she could move, Merry slipped out from the cover of the bush and sneaked into the Academy kitchens, leaving Gabrielle feeling completely baffled.

A few moments later, Merry crept out of the kitchen again, clutching a bunch of carrots and a cabbage. She hid behind one bush, then another as she attempted to slip out of the garden.

But Angel Carmel, the school cook,

came flying out of the kitchen at top speed, calling furiously: "Who took my vegetables? I'll get you…!"

Gabrielle saw Angel Carmel come right up to the bush where Merry was hiding.

"Please don't find her," she mouthed silently into the night air.

"Where are you?" stormed Angel Carmel. "And who are you? I can smell those vegetables! I know you're not some fox. Why are you stealing from us, eh? This is an Angel Academy, not a school for young rogues, though it's hard to believe at times."

Merry kept absolutely still, but Gabrielle could see the edges of her wings sticking out from behind the bush. *Oh dear, Angel*

Carmel is bound to spot her, thought Gabrielle, holding her breath.

As Carmel swept past the bush, Gabrielle had to hide her eyes with her hands, she was so sure Merry would be found. But needing to know what was happening, Gabrielle opened her fingers and peeked out just in time to see Angel Carmel pass by Merry without spotting her.

Gabrielle sighed with relief.

Carmel turned and headed back into the kitchen, muttering under her breath: "Cheeky as they come – stealing vegetables indeed. Don't I feed them enough?"

Phew! What a lucky escape! thought Gabrielle.

She watched as Merry emerged nervously from the bush, looking this way and that, as if she expected to be grabbed by the neck at any moment. Then she took to the sky, with the stolen vegetables hidden beneath her cloak.

Gabrielle wondered whether to go after her, but Merry flew away so quickly, Gabrielle knew she'd never be able to catch her up. She decided to head back to Crystals instead, puzzling over what she had seen.

Gabrielle saw Merry the next day after breakfast and they managed to snatch a conversation on the way to their first lesson – Potion-making with Angel Blossom.

"I'm sorry I couldn't meet you last night," said Merry.

"I waited for ages," Gabrielle replied, looking at her friend worriedly.

"I did plan to meet you, honestly," said Merry. "I just had to do something first and then I had to dash…"

"I saw you," said Gabrielle.

"Oh no! Where were you?"

"I was watching from the kitchen garden wall. Angel Carmel was very angry. You were lucky that you didn't get caught," said Gabrielle.

"I know," Merry nodded. "I was being a bit silly."

"What were the vegetables for?" asked Gabrielle. "Surely you weren't hungry."

"I can't tell you," Merry began in a whisper. "Last night really spooked me and it's not fair to involve you. If I get into trouble, that's fine. But I'm not dragging you into this as well."

"But, Merry, I really want to help you," said Gabrielle. "Whatever is making you do all these crazy things – is it really worth it?"

"Yes, completely," said Merry. "They mean everything to me."

"Who mean everything to you?" asked Gabrielle.

"Please, don't ask any more questions, I beg you," said Merry under her breath. "I'll sort this out, I promise."

"Believe me, it's horrid being in trouble with Madame Seraph, and I should know," worried Gabrielle.

"That's why I can't involve you," said Merry. "It wouldn't be fair. You had a bad enough time with Lula!"

Gabrielle had gone through a terrible time with an older Cherubic called Lula Spendlove. Lula had been jealous of Gabrielle's Earth Angel status when she'd first arrived and had got Gabrielle into serious trouble. Being at Angel Academy meant everything to Gabrielle and she never wanted to go through anything like that again, but Merry seemed to be getting herself into deeper and deeper trouble; Gabrielle felt she couldn't stand by and watch that happen. She just had to find out what was going on, because Merry obviously needed help.

Chapter 9

In Crystals that evening, the four room-
mates chatted excitedly about their
Vanishing lesson the next morning. So far
in lessons they'd learned about the theory
of vanishing and why being able to become
invisible was so important to Guardian
Angels, but tomorrow they were going on
an outing to find their own vanishing
crystal. They would bring the crystal back

to the school, then grind it down into a vanishing powder so that they could put the theory into practice. Gabrielle was very excited to think she might soon be able to vanish whenever she wanted. But she was also a little worried. Her biggest fear was that she might not become visible again.

The next morning after breakfast in the Ambroserie, the Cherubics were told to collect a packed lunch on their way out.

"I wonder where we'll go?" said Gabrielle, as they flew to the stables to meet Angel Peter, the Vanishing Arts teacher, and their chevalanges.

"To the Vanishing River, of course," said Ruth. "Because that's where you get vanishing crystals."

"Oooh, that sounds amazing," laughed Gabrielle.

At the stables, the girls were met by Angel Raphael, who helped them to prepare their chevalanges for the long journey. Then, once the horses were ready, Angel Peter took over, sitting up straight astride his magnificent chevalange, Indigo.

"Cherubics," he began, "today you will travel with me to the outer edges of Cloud Nimbus to visit Vanishing River. Once there, we will select crystals to bring 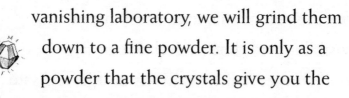 back to the Academy. Then, in my vanishing laboratory, we will grind them down to a fine powder. It is only as a powder that the crystals give you the power to vanish," Angel Peter explained.

"At this stage of your schooling, only I have the authority to make you invisible and bring you back to visibility," he continued gravely. "Making the powder is a delicate procedure, though the spell itself is simple enough. However, I can see from your faces how eager you are to get started, and I must warn you that there will be serious consequences for any Cherubics found using the powder without full training."

He glanced around. "We know how much fun you can have making yourselves invisible, but it's not always so easy to regain visibility. We will work on vanishing for the rest of this term and on regaining visibility next term. After one or two unfortunate incidents in the past, it has been agreed that all Cherubics must undergo training in how and when to use vanishing before you are allowed to practise on your own. Now I shall require all of you to behave perfectly and listen to my instructions. Is that quite clear?"

"Yes, Angel Peter," chimed the Cherubics. Despite his warning, they were almost dancing with excitement.

The trainee angels flew up onto their chevalanges and, with Angel Peter leading the way, the group swept majestically westwards in a flurry of flapping wings and flowing cloaks, over the snowy town of Bliss.

They were flying further than Gabrielle had flown before. What an adventure! For the first time, she would be able to see the remote parts of Cloud Nimbus, and from a bird's-eye point-of-view, which was by far the best way.

At first they could see little further than the snow-covered fields which lay just beyond the town. But these gave way to wilder scenery, with snow-capped, purple hills and curious, silver trees. Before long, Gabrielle could see a wide, gushing river.

"That's the Vanishing River," said Domino.

"Wow! It's shimmering!" cried Gabrielle, amazed.

"It is, isn't it?" said Domino.

"But how do we find the crystals?" she asked, as they prepared to land.

"You're all going 'fishing' for them. It's great fun to search for the crystals as they flow along with the rush of the water!" Domino explained. "They are constantly being made in the river, so don't worry, you're sure to find some."

"But it will be so cold," said Gabrielle.

"Ah, that's where you're wrong," smiled
Domino. "I know it's snowy, but the river is
always warm – it stays at the perfect
temperature for the crystals to develop."

Gabrielle couldn't wait to begin her
search.

Up ahead, Angel Peter raised his arm
and slowed the group. "Prepare to land,"
he called. The chevalanges
swooped to the ground, and
the excited Cherubics
jumped from their backs and
rushed to the snowy riverbank.
Gabrielle was stunned by the
exquisite beauty of this mystical part
of Cloud Nimbus. Trees curved around one

another and over the river, as though in deep conversation. The water twinkled in the wintry sunlight; it seemed shot through with rainbow-hued crystals. Gabrielle guessed these were the vanishing crystals they would be collecting.

It was so beautiful and peaceful here, Gabrielle suddenly felt all her anxiety evaporate away.

"Gather round, Cherubics," Angel Peter called. The girls looked on expectantly as their Vanishing Arts teacher showed them how to fish for crystals, using special nets with long handles. He'd brought a net for each Cherubic.

This is just like fishing with Dad and Grandpa! thought Gabrielle, as she hovered above the water holding her net out in front of her. *Only, we never used to catch any fish.*

"Look for a crystal that will fit into the palm of your hand," said Angel Peter. "That will give you enough powder to use until the end of term. And don't be greedy – take only one crystal each."

The Cherubics had great fun hovering above the river, waiting to capture the prettiest crystals. But the task was not easy! Silver-spangled fish shimmied along in the water, and the crystals themselves bobbed along the surface teasingly, then seemed to slip away when any of the finely meshed nets came close to capturing them.

For a time, it seemed as if no one had the correct technique. But soon

one Cherubic after another began to get
it right.

"Got one!" called Ruth. When Ruth
decided to concentrate on something,
she was usually very good at it.

Her luck made Gabrielle even more
determined to get her own crystal, but
the harder she tried, the worse she did.
It was like trying to catch a slippery fish
with your fingers – there was nothing
to grip.

"How ever did you manage it?" she
called to Ruth.

"It's easy," Ruth laughed. "Get

 your eye on one particular
crystal, follow it and
don't let it out of your sight!
Then bring your net down

on it," she advised, as she brandished her own crystal proudly in her hand.

Before long most of the Cherubics had snagged a vanishing crystal, and Gabrielle became flustered that she still didn't have one.

Ruth, who had been giving advice to some of the others, came over to help her. "Right, let's focus on this sparkly one coming downstream now. It's winking at us," she said. "Hold the net steady…place it in front of the crystal…good. Hold firm. Don't be nervous. Steady! It's in there! Well done!"

"Yay! I've got one!" squealed Gabrielle, taking the shimmering crystal out of the net and holding it in her palm. "It's so sparkly! I love it. Thanks, Ruth – you're brilliant."

"Yes, I suppose I am," laughed Ruth.

Now that everyone had successfully snagged a crystal, Angel Peter addressed the group again. "Well done, Cherubics. As everyone has their crystal, let's have lunch, then we'll return to the Academy and set to work making our powder in the lab. Then you'll each get the chance to perform a short vanishing exercise."

"I can't wait to try it out," said Gabrielle, making sure her crystal was safely in her cloak pocket.

"Same here!" said Ruth, patting both her pockets and smiling broadly.

Chapter 10

Back in Angel Peter's vanishing lab, Gabrielle and Ruth listened carefully to the instructions about grinding down the crystal, and watched as Angel Peter ground down each stone in turn. Once the powders were ready, they were placed in small jars, each labelled with a Cherubic's name.

"Now, girls," said Angel Peter, "please form a line to collect your jar of powder.

I shall sprinkle each of you in turn with your own powder and say the word 'Disparu'. You will then vanish for a few seconds, until I make you visible again with a drop of visibility potion!"

Ruth dashed to the front of the queue, calling, "Me first! Me first!" while Gabrielle hovered nervously at the back, suddenly anxious at the thought of being made invisible.

"Does anyone have any questions?" asked Peter.

"Yes," said Ruth. "Can we get stuck in the invisible mode?"

"No. The visibility potion has never failed when I have used it. I will say the word 'Apparu' as I sprinkle it on you. That always does the trick!"

Gabrielle watched carefully as Angel Peter took a set of keys from his desk drawer, unlocked a cabinet and picked out a bottle labelled *Visibility Potion*.

"Ready?" he asked.

"One last question," said Ruth. "Will you be able to hear me talk when I have vanished?"

"Yes, alas, we will!" joked the teacher.

"I'd better not say anything rude then!" giggled Ruth. "Okay. I'm ready now!" she said, turning to give a thumbs up to Gabrielle, as she grinned from ear to ear.

Gabrielle was full of admiration for her friend as she stood bravely, waiting to be the first in the class to disappear.

"Disparu, Ruth Bell!" said Peter. He raised a hand above Ruth's head and rubbed his thumb and forefinger to release a sprinkling of shimmering powder.

Gabrielle held her breath and closed her eyes for a split second. When she opened them, Ruth was nowhere to be seen. "Ruth!" she called. "Ruth! Are you there?"

"Yes, and I'm fine. I can see all of you but I can't see myself! It's not scary though, it's fun!" giggled Ruth. "I'm making a face at Angel Peter right now!"

"Very funny," said Peter. "I'm going to make you visible again, so I can see what you're up to! Come here please and take my hand."

He sprinkled the visibility potion over what seemed to be thin air at the same time as he said the word "Apparu", and immediately Ruth reappeared.

"That was super-brilliant!" she said.

Gabrielle fidgeted from one foot to the other as she waited for her turn. She wished she shared Ruth's sense of adventure, and was cross with herself for feeling so nervous.

All the other Cherubics vanished and were made visible again – it looked so easy. Even Merry, who seemed painfully tired, went through it all without a problem. And as soon as she was visible again, Merry asked when the Cherubics would be allowed to vanish on their own. Angel Peter raised an eyebrow at that and told her she'd have to be patient as there was still a lot to learn.

At last, it was Gabrielle's turn. She stood nervously in front of Angel Peter

as he took a pinch of her powder and
raised his hand.

"Okay, Gabrielle?" he asked.

"Erm, I think so… But…has there
ever been an angel who didn't come back?
I mean, I'm only part-angel – what if it's
different for me?"

"Gabrielle," Angel Peter smiled at her,
"Earth Angels have exactly the same
powers as pure angels, if not more. I
promise, as long as I'm here, you'll be fine."

"Okay, then, I'm ready!" she said,
screwing up her eyes.

"Disparu, Gabrielle Divine!" he said.

Gabrielle held her breath. She didn't
know whether she had vanished or not.
"Can you see me?" she asked, casting her
eyes around the room.

"No, we can't see you!" said Peter.

"This is so funny. Can I walk right through you?" she said.

"No, you are hidden from sight, but your body is still solid, so you can only do the things you'd normally do when you're visible," said Peter.

Gabrielle raced up to people who clearly could not see her. She tried whispering in their ear, and she tickled Ruth. Their reactions were so funny. It was a weird sensation, but she loved it!

"Time to bring you back now," said the teacher.

"Oh, so soon?" said Gabrielle.

"Hah! You've changed your tune!" he said, holding out his hand in the direction of her voice. "Take my hand," he instructed.

"Apparu, Gabrielle Divine!"
He released a few drops of the potion and
she was visible again!

Gabrielle giggled with relief. "That
wasn't so bad!" she said.

"Told you!" said Ruth. "You did really
well!"

"Now, you all need to give me your jars
of vanishing powder and I will lock them up
safely in my cabinet. We don't want anyone
vanishing without permission. I'll say it
again: vanishing can be a very dangerous
thing to do without supervision," Angel
Peter said sternly.

Chapter 11

The day of the Chevallet test for the Chevalange Charm was drawing nearer and Gabrielle was busy preparing. All the Cherubics had been given extra time at the stables to work with their chevalanges.

"I can't believe it's actually happening tomorrow! I'm so nervous!" said Gabrielle.

The girls all went down to the stables in the afternoon to rehearse their routines with their chevalanges and the school orchestra one last time. When it was their turn, Gabrielle and Domino flew elegantly across the lawns, working on the finishing touches to their dance, as the orchestra accompanied them with their chosen piece of music.

Afterwards, Gabrielle groomed Domino until his coat shone, braiding his mane and tying the end of each braid with white satin ribbon. As for his tack, she polished the deep tan saddle with beeswax and cleaned each gemstone on his dress bridle until it dazzled. While she was busy, Merry's chevalange, Posy, popped her head over the tack-room door to ask whether Gabrielle had seen Merry.

Gabrielle was puzzled. "I've not seen her since lunchtime, but I assumed she was down here running through her routine with you."

"She should be," said Posy, looking anxious. "We're never going to be ready to perform tomorrow. Merry just doesn't seem to be taking the Chevallet test seriously. There's something very wrong, but she won't tell me what it is."

"I know," Gabrielle said, stroking Posy's silky mane, "she won't tell me either but, whatever it is, it's getting out of hand."

Gabrielle and her friends were tired after their long day, and starving hungry, so they tucked into a delicious dinner in the Ambroserie, chatting all the while about the Chevallet test and about the mystery surrounding Merry. Afterwards they headed up to Crystals together.

With so much going on, Gabrielle was exhausted, and after a soak in a warm lavender bath, she felt she couldn't stay awake another minute. "I'm going to have an early night so I'm fresh for the routine tomorrow," she said.

"Okay, see you in the morning," said Ruth. "Goodnight."

"Goodnight, Gabrielle!" said the twins.

"Sleep well," called Sylvie.

Gabrielle snuggled into her fluffy quilt, and fell into a blissful, deep sleep.

During the night, she woke up suddenly. At first, she couldn't think what had disturbed her. She pulled her quilt around her, and tried to settle down. But she was disturbed again. This time, she was sure she heard her name being called.

"Gabrielle, Gabrielle!" whispered Sylvie in her ear. "Wake up! Please!"

Gabrielle woke up fully this time, with a start. "What is it, Sylvie?" she asked.

"It's Ruth! She's not in her bed!"

Gabrielle rubbed her sleepy eyes and tried to make sense of what Sylvie had said.

"Can you check in the bathroom?" asked Sylvie.

Gabrielle jumped up and ran to the bathroom, wondering whether Ruth was feeling all right. But there was no sign of her. She came back into the bedroom and went over to Ruth's bed, desperately searching for a clue as to where she might be. She saw that Ruth had put pillows under her quilt, to make it look like she was asleep, so whatever she was doing had obviously been planned.

As Gabrielle searched around, she spotted a little dish on Ruth's bedside cabinet. There were traces of shimmering powder in it…

"What's this?" said Gabrielle.

Sylvie flew over to look and sighed.

"Oh, no. Are you thinking what I'm thinking?" asked Gabrielle.

"Vanishing powder?" said Sylvie.

"Yes, but how did she get it?" wondered Gabrielle, thinking as fast as her half-asleep brain would allow. "We had to leave our jars of powder with Angel Peter."

"Who knows what Ruth is up to?" Sylvie

shook her little head. "We've got to find her."

Gabrielle began to panic. "You know what this means, don't you, Sylvie?"

"Trouble!" said Sylvie.

"She's…she's disappeared!" said Gabrielle with a gulping sob. "How will we find her if we can't see her?"

"But how did she manage to make herself disappear? Angel Peter is always careful to lock up all the vanishing powder," said the little dove.

Gabrielle suddenly realized what Ruth might have done. "Oh, I have a feeling I know. It would have been easy for her to take an extra crystal from the river! She was super-quick at catching them and, come to think of it, she seemed to have something in both pockets of her cloak at the end of the session."

"Oh, that girl!" said Sylvie crossly. "Sometimes I despair of her, really I do. How does she think we're going to get her back to visibility without involving Angel Peter, and therefore Madame Seraph? The visibility potion is always locked up in a cabinet too."

"Let's think," said Gabrielle. "She was here when I went to bed but I've been sleeping for ages, so I have no idea when she vanished. When did you last see her?"

"I'm not sure," said Sylvie. "The rest of you were asleep, but Ruth was still pottering around the room. I was sitting on the windowsill, and I spotted Merry Harper sneaking off again. I turned round and told Ruth about it. Then…well, that's actually the last time I heard or saw her!"

"It's not like you to miss someone leaving the room," said Gabrielle.

"I know," agreed Sylvie. "But I was very concerned about Merry and wondering whether I should report her to Madame Seraph. Ruth must have made herself invisible, then left. It was only when I was doing my midnight checks that I realized she was missing."

"I wonder if she went after Merry?" said Gabrielle. "I know she wants to find out what's going on as much as I do."

"Oh, of course, you're probably right," agreed Sylvie.

Gabrielle didn't know what to do. It was

going to be impossible to search for an invisible angel, but it wasn't in her nature to ignore the situation.

"Let's go and check round the grounds," said Gabrielle. "I know we won't be able to see her, but we can call her name. I just have to hope Madame Seraph doesn't see us!" She grabbed her velvet cloak and put it on over her nightdress, then pulled on her cosy outdoor boots.

"We shouldn't be doing this," said Sylvie anxiously, from her perch on the windowsill. "But I'll sit here and keep watch until you're outside, then I'll come and join you."

Gabrielle floated through the school and slipped out of the back door, trying not to think about the last time she and Ruth had snuck out at this time of night. Earlier in the term they had gone out to practise flying over the lake. Gabrielle had got into so much trouble! She shuddered at the thought, but there was no going back now. She had to try and find Ruth.

Sylvie fluttered over to join her and the two of them flew over the gardens, the lawns and along the edges of the lake, quietly calling out for Ruth. There was no reply.

"Let's check the courtyard and the turrets," suggested Gabrielle.

There was still no response to their calls.

"I wonder if she's gone to see Humphrey at the stables?" said Gabrielle, searching her brain for ideas.

"If she had gone there, the chevalanges

would have raised the alarm very quickly," said Sylvie.

"Yes, that's true," Gabrielle agreed.

"You shouldn't be out here either," said the little bird, "it's far too risky. I think all we can do now is go back to Crystals and wait for Ruth to come to us."

Gabrielle was crazy with worry and when she got back to the room, she shook Hope gently awake.

"Hope. Hope," she whispered. "Ruth has gone missing and we think she might have made herself vanish!"

"Oh no!" said Hope sleepily. "What are we going to do?"

"I don't know. We've given up searching outside. Now we're hoping she'll come back here soon. And then we'll have to think about how we can bring her back to visibility again!" said Gabrielle.

"What can I do to help?" asked Hope.

"What can any of us do?" Gabrielle answered.

Sylvie started muttering that it was her duty to tell Madame Seraph that Ruth was missing. Gabrielle was beside herself with worry and begged Sylvie to hold on a little longer. However, at that moment, Gabrielle heard a whisper in her ear, which made her jump: "Gabrielle, it's me. I'm standing next to you!"

It was Ruth!

"Oh, thank goodness!" cried Gabrielle. "How long have you been here?"

"I've just come back," said Ruth.

"But what have you been doing? We've

been so worried. I was beginning to think
you were never going to turn up," said
Gabrielle, feeling rather silly speaking into
thin air.

"Sorry," said Ruth.

"You've had us all in a flap," said Hope.
"Why did you make yourself invisible?"

"I just got this idea into my head to take
an extra crystal when we were at the
Vanishing River. I ground it down to
powder in the lab but didn't give it to Angel
Peter. And when Sylvie mentioned that
Merry was behaving oddly again, I decided
to see if the powder would work, so I could
spy on her and see where she keeps
disappearing off to. I didn't for a second
think saying 'Disparu' to myself would
make me vanish, but it did. It was so easy!"

"I can't believe you tried it after Angel Peter's warning," scolded Gabrielle. "You're crazy."

"I know," said Ruth sorrowfully. "I always seem to see how silly I am after I've done these things. It seemed like such a good idea at the time."

"Did you find Merry?" asked Hope.

"Yes and it was going really well – I even saw where she went. But she locked the door behind her and I couldn't get in, because like Angel Peter said, my body was still solid. Then when Merry came out, she locked the door again, so I couldn't see what was inside," explained Ruth.

"So, where did she go?" asked Gabrielle.

"To a barn at the bottom of the gardens! I've never even noticed it before," said Ruth.

"Did you find anything out?" asked Hope.

"Not much, because, as I said, I couldn't get in there. But maybe together we could find a way in…" Ruth suggested.

"Well, we could, but right now you should be worrying about how you are going to become visible again before breakfast," said Gabrielle.

"Erm, you're right," admitted Ruth. "And I'm not sure. I didn't exactly think it through, did I?"

Sylvie shook her head in despair. "I think I'm going to have to tell Madame Seraph. We need help."

"Oh, Sylvie, Ruth will be in so much trouble. Give us a few more minutes," Gabrielle pleaded. "There has to be a way."

Sylvie nodded her little head and went to her perch on the windowsill to think things through.

"We've got to do something," Hope said, "but what?"

At that point, Charity woke up. "What's going on? Who are you talking to?" she asked.

"It's Ruth," said Gabrielle.

"I can't see her," said Charity. "Where is she?"

"She's vanished," said Hope, flopping down on her sister's bed.

"She's done what?!" said Charity, sitting bolt upright.

Gabrielle knew that Charity would think Ruth had been ridiculous – but together, maybe they could help their friend reappear before she got into terrible trouble.

Chapter 12

Gabrielle told Charity what had happened.

"Yes, you heard right," she said. "She's here...but she's not here."

"I'm definitely here," Ruth butted in. "You just can't see me."

"How stupid is that! How are we going to get you back?" asked Charity.

"That's just what we were wondering," said Gabrielle. "If the teachers find out what she's done, she'll probably be sent home! Sylvie thinks we should tell Madame Seraph, but we don't want Ruth to get into trouble. Are there any tips in your vanishing book, Charity?"

"Well, we can't do anything without Angel Peter's visibility potion!" said Charity.

"But it's locked away in his lab," said Hope.

"I could get it," Gabrielle volunteered.

"No, you mustn't get into trouble again. You look after Ruth here while Hope and I go and get it," said Charity.

Ruth stepped in at this point. "Girls, you're all being fantastic. Thanks so much!" she said. "I don't deserve you! But there is an obvious answer here: I should go and get the potion myself – after all, no one will see me."

"No, Ruth, you stay here," said Charity, swinging her legs over the edge of her bed. "We don't want you getting into any more trouble either. Nobody must find out what you've done. Come on, Hope, you can keep watch while I go into Angel Peter's lab and get his keys, then I'll take a few drops of the potion from his cabinet. I'll try and do the 'Apparu' thing when we get back, with the help of my vanishing book. Fingers crossed, you'll be visible again in a blink!"

"That sounds like a brilliant plan," said Ruth. "Thank you, Charity. I'm so sorry you're having to break the rules for me."

"You're worth it," said Charity. "I know

you'd do the same for Hope and me."

The twins got ready at super-quick speed and sneaked out of Crystals as quietly as they could. Sylvie, Gabrielle and Ruth chatted quietly while they waited for them to return.

"Have you any idea what Merry is up to?" asked Gabrielle. "If only we could help her."

"I don't know," answered Ruth. "But if we could get into that barn we might find out. Whatever it is, she has to stop this crazy behaviour."

"I wish we could get her to confide in us. It's the end of term soon, and she can't behave like this next term too or she'll make herself ill, or get into terrible trouble, or both!"

Waiting for the twins to come back seemed to take an eternity. Gabrielle began to pace around anxiously, while Sylvie hopped along the windowsill in a distracted state. "I should tell Madame," she kept mumbling to herself. "I really should tell Madame."

"Oh, Sylvie, I know it's hard for you, but please don't," pleaded Gabrielle.

"Something's gone wrong, I just know it!" Sylvie said.

At last, the door of Crystals opened. The twins had returned with a small amount of the potion in a test tube. Now it was time to make Ruth reappear.

Charity opened her book and studied it carefully for a moment. "Ruth, you'll need to come and stand in front of me since I can't see you," Charity instructed.

"Okay," said Ruth's disembodied voice.
"I'm here, Charity. Let's go for it."

The others held their breath as
Charity sprinkled the visibility
potion over the invisible Ruth,
saying "Apparu, Ruth Bell," as
she did so.

It worked! Ruth was visible at last, with
her wild red hair bouncing around her
shoulders, and a beaming smile
on her warm, freckly face.

"Ruth!" cried Gabrielle, leaning
over to hug her friend. "It's lovely
to see you again!"

"Oh, it's so nice to be back. I had no
idea how I was going to sort this. But
everything's normal again thanks to you

two!" said Ruth, embracing the twins.

"This time, we got away without involving the teachers," said Charity, eyeing Ruth peevishly, "but that's the first and last time I put myself at risk after one of your mad ideas!"

"I second that!" said Sylvie.

"I understand," said Ruth. "I know it seems silly to you! But I was only trying to be a good angel. I really wanted to help Merry."

"You can't worry about Merry just now, girls," chirped Sylvie. "Have you noticed the time?"

The four girls gasped. They couldn't be late for breakfast! They quickly got ready to head for the Ambroserie.

"Thanks, Sylvie," Gabrielle called before

she raced through the door.

"I won't be able to keep any more secrets," the little dove worried.

"I know," replied Gabrielle. "I'm just so relieved Ruth is back. Now all we have to do is pass the Chevallet test – and find out what's going on with Merry."

Chapter 13

With the test taking place later on that morning, the Chevallet routine should have been the main thing on Gabrielle's mind, but as they arrived at the Ambroserie, she looked all around until she spotted Merry.

"I have an idea which might get Merry to tell us what she's up to," she whispered to Ruth.

"Okay," said Ruth. "Let's go and sit with her."

While the twins went to their favourite seats, Gabrielle and Ruth made their way over to Merry.

"Hi, Merry," said Gabrielle. "Can we join you?"

"Yes, that'd be nice," said Merry, rubbing her sleepy eyes.

Gabrielle and Ruth sat down and pulled their seats up close.

"Merry," whispered Gabrielle. "We were in the grounds last night, and we saw you in the barn. We know your secret!" It was a little fib, but Gabrielle hoped it would make Merry feel able to discuss her problems.

"Oh, do you?" said Merry, sounding

worried. "Oh dear, I didn't want anyone else to find out. It's too dangerous."

"But you look worn out. We only want to help," said Gabrielle kindly.

Merry suddenly looked relieved. "Okay," she said, "we haven't got time now because of the Chevallet test. I'm so behind with my routine. I need to go and have one more practice. Meet me at the barn after we've done our routines and I'll show them to you!"

"Great!" said Gabrielle. "See you there. Now have a huge breakfast. You need plenty of energy!"

"Don't worry, I'm having a bit of everything," said Merry. "And sneaking some stuff for them too," she added under her breath, as she pointed to a little bag

under the table, crammed full of fruit and
oats.

As they left the table, Ruth winked at
Gabrielle. "Well done!" she said.

"Phew, I'm glad she didn't ask what
we'd seen in the barn!" said Gabrielle.
"I still have no idea."

Back at Crystals, Sylvie had Good
Luck cards for all four girls from their
parents.

Gabrielle opened the card from Mum
and Dad.

*Do your best, little angel. We're sure
Domino will assist you well with the
Chevallet test. We're so proud of you,
and we have lots of exciting things planned
for your Christmas holiday! See you soon,*

darling. Love you always, Mum and Dad,

xxxx

It was lovely to hear from her parents, but Gabrielle suddenly felt sick with nerves. *What if I don't do well in the Chevallet test and don't earn the charm?* she thought. The worst thing would be for the other Cherubics to have the pretty charm dangling from their bracelets, while she had nothing at all. And of course, she would be so disappointed to miss out on meeting the Snow Angel.

The Cherubics got changed for their performances. They helped one another to zip up the satin bodices of their white tutus, and stepped into their satin ballet shoes, tying the ribbons carefully. "No one

wants a ballet shoe falling from the air
mid-dance!" said Charity. "Let's
do a treble bow!"

They styled their hair in high
ballet buns and wrapped their fleece cloaks
around their shoulders to keep out the
winter chill. Then they headed down to the
stables, chattering all the way.

"I'm so excited about this," said
Gabrielle. "I hope everyone likes our
routine! But I can't help wondering what
Merry's been doing in that barn!"

"Same here," said Ruth. "But we'll find
out soon enough. We've got to focus on
the Chevallet for now."

"Apparently Mademoiselle Balance,
the examiner from the Chevallet
Headquarters, has arrived!" said Charity,

who'd been talking to another very anxious Cherubic.

"I hope she's not strict!" said Gabrielle nervously.

"You've got nothing to worry about, Gabrielle," said Ruth. "You're brilliant at this."

Down at the stables, Domino tried his best to put Gabrielle at ease.

"Relax," he said, as Gabrielle brushed his coat. "We're going to earn this charm! You'll see. You've created a lovely Chevallet routine!"

"I feel as if I'll mess up the moves, or do something really stupid!" said Gabrielle.

"When have you ever messed them up before?" laughed Domino.

"Never. I know. I just panic. I'm an idiot, sorry!"

"It's natural to be anxious, but you'll be fine!" said Domino reassuringly. "And I'll be with you every step of the way."

At last Angel Raphael and Angel Anna arrived with Madame Seraph and the rather severe-looking examiner; it was time for the Chevallet routines to begin, out on the snow-covered paddock. The majestic chevalanges stood proudly in a line, their coats gleaming and their jewelled bridles twinkling. Each one carried a beautiful Cherubic on its back. The whole sight was breathtaking.

The school orchestra was assembled under a large gazebo, ready to accompany each Chevallet routine. Gabrielle felt a burst of pride and a tinge of regret: she wished that her mum and dad could see it all.

Angel Raphael addressed the Cherubics. "Good morning, everyone. I'm sure you'd all like to join me in welcoming Mademoiselle Balance to our Academy." Following the teacher's lead, the Cherubics all clapped their hands in welcome.

Mademoiselle Balance smiled graciously which, Gabrielle thought, made her look a little less severe.

Angel Raphael continued, "We will now watch each pair's Chevallet display, so when I call your names please come forward and take up your starting positions. You've all worked extremely hard on your routines and I'm sure each and every one of you is capable of earning the Chevalange

Charm today. Good luck, and enjoy your chance to shine!"

As the orchestra struck up, the atmosphere became tense and Gabrielle began to quiver with nerves. She watched her fellow Cherubics anxiously, waiting for her turn. At the final rehearsal, Angel Raphael and Angel Anna had read out the order for the performances. Gabrielle and Domino were going to perform last. Gabrielle's heart had sunk at the thought of having to wait so long and now she was becoming increasingly nervous. Mademoiselle Balance was making lots of notes in a little black book. It really was a serious business and Gabrielle started to worry that she had not put in enough practice.

Gabrielle chewed her lip as she waited,

watching pair after pair complete their Chevallet routines. Ruth's piece was adventurous and fun, Charity's serious and technically perfect, whilst Hope's was lively and playful. Gabrielle forgot her own worries as Merry and Posy were called forward. They both looked anxious and uncertain, but after a hesitant start, they really got into their stride. Gabrielle cheered her friends; they had all done so well, and she was especially pleased for Merry.

Suddenly, her name was being called: "Gabrielle Divine on Domino, please," said Angel Raphael. The pair took up their starting position and waited for the orchestra to begin. Gabrielle was shaking all over but Domino remained calm and gradually his confidence filtered through

to Gabrielle. They worked beautifully together, spinning and leaping in unison, with their wings flapping at the same time. Their hardest move, the grande jeté, where Gabrielle and Domino both jumped through the air, but reconnected at the end, went perfectly. Gabrielle heard applause below and began to relax into the performance.
Phew, it's going well, she thought, as they executed the spins, twists and swoops with ease.

But as the routine was coming to an end and Domino began to descend, Gabrielle became aware of a commotion below. Now, instead of watching her routine, the Cherubics and chevalanges on the ground seemed to be staring at some lumps of snow in the paddock.

Distracted, Gabrielle tried to look down from her seat on Domino's back to see what was going on. She was close enough now to her audience to hear Hope as she blurted out, "Oh look! The snow is hopping."

For a moment Gabrielle forgot all about the examiner. She gazed in disbelief at the commotion below her. The snow was hopping. She couldn't believe her eyes. *But maybe it is possible,* she thought. *We are on Cloud Nimbus after all. Anything can happen here.* But as Domino circled the paddock, looking for a safe place to land, Gabrielle realized that the snow wasn't hopping at all. Instead, everyone was looking at a group of pure white rabbits.

Chapter 14

Gabrielle smiled with delight. A pure white mother rabbit and nine little bunnies were hopping happily across the snow beneath her!

Down on the ground she heard Ruth call out, "Oh, how sweet! It's a rabbit family!"

"My babies! How did you get out of the barn, you little rascals?" Gabrielle saw Merry run forward and scoop up the mother rabbit in her arms, hugging her tightly.

Once Merry had gathered up all the baby rabbits, Domino thought it was safe to land. Gabrielle couldn't wait to join the other Cherubics on the ground, but just as they touched down, Madame Seraph called for silence. In all the excitement, Gabrielle had forgotten that Merry was most likely in very big trouble.

"Cherubics," the Head Angel said, "this is most unusual and I can only apologize to Mademoiselle Balance for the disruption to our Chevallet test…"

But the examiner's stern face seemed to have melted. Even she couldn't resist the cute little bunnies! "Well, it's certainly been a memorable morning," said Mademoiselle

Balance, "and I can see there is going to be chaos here for some time to come, so why don't I go away and talk to Angel Raphael and Angel Anna about the Cherubics' routines. Then I'll announce the results shortly."

"Hurray!" cried the girls gleefully.

After hugs from their trainee angels, the chevalanges went back to the stables to rest, and all the Cherubics flew to help Merry gather up the baby rabbits, who kept escaping from her.

"So this is what you've been doing in the barn!" said Gabrielle, delighted she understood Merry's mystery at last.

"I thought you two knew?" said Merry.

"Oh," laughed Ruth. "We were bluffing! We knew you were hiding something in the barn, but we didn't know what."

"Nice try!" said Merry. "But my secret's out now!"

"I'm surprised you managed to keep it for so long," said Gabrielle.

"I simply had to," said Merry. "You know how we're not allowed pets, but I couldn't bear to be parted from Anoushka, the mother rabbit, so when term started I brought her here and hid her in the barn. She lived quite happily in an old box and never moved from it unless I lifted her out."

"Weren't you scared that someone would find out?" asked Gabrielle.

"Yes, I was, and when the babies were born, I got a big shock. I had to get such a lot of food and bedding for them all. That's what I'd bought when you saw me at the Wintervale Fair. And I had to build a hutch, because they kept racing around and escaping from the barn. That's what the driftwood from the river was for," Merry explained.

"It's all starting to make sense now," said Ruth.

"You see, I can't live without Anoushka, and I didn't want her sent away with the babies, so I had to look after all of them. I'm the only person who knows how to care for them and what they all like," said Merry, as she cuddled Anoushka.

"That's the sweetest story I've ever heard, but poor you," said Gabrielle. "No wonder you've been so stressed! Ten bunnies relying on you!"

Madame Seraph made her way over
to the little group of Cherubics huddled
around Merry.

"Now, Merry dear," she said sternly,
"pets are strictly forbidden at Angel
Academy, but these bunnies look cold.
Let's help you take them back to the barn
before they freeze! Then we will discuss
what's to be done with them and with you."

While Madame Seraph's tone was
disapproving, Gabrielle was very relieved
that she didn't seem furious with Merry.
There was something about the bunnies
that had melted everyone's hearts.

"I'm sorry, Madame Seraph," said Merry.
"I know I've done wrong, but I love them
so much!"

Gabrielle bent down and picked up the

smallest baby bunny, who was straggling behind her brothers and sisters. The tiny white ball of fur snuggled into her, and looked up with grateful midnight-blue eyes.

"You are lovely!" said Gabrielle, kissing the bunny's cold little nose. "I wonder what you're called. You look to me like a 'Snowdrop'."

As the Cherubics helped to settle the rabbits back in the barn, Gabrielle and Ruth noticed the straw and hay from the Fair, bags of carrots and cabbage leaves from the kitchen, as well as a makeshift wooden hutch, built using the driftwood from the river. It seemed so obvious now why Merry had been hiding things under her cloak for the last three weeks.

"Merry has done a great job of looking after the rabbits," said Ruth.

"I wish we could have helped her," said Gabrielle. "They are so adorable. Especially Snowdrop. I wonder why she didn't want us to know."

"I suppose she just thought that if she told anyone there was more chance of the teachers finding out," said Ruth. "Madame Seraph will never allow her to keep them here."

"But it's such a shame that we won't be able to see them next term!" said Gabrielle, tucking Snowdrop into a cosy bed of straw.

Once the rabbits were secured in the barn, Angel Raphael flew over to Madame Seraph and handed her some notes.

"Cherubics," she called, "I'd like you all

to fly over to the stables to join your chevalanges, as Mademoiselle Balance has an important announcement to make."

There was an excited buzz in the air as the Cherubics flew to the stables, where the chevalanges were waiting impatiently to be reunited with their partners.

Once everyone was gathered together, Mademoiselle Balance stood in front of them. "I just wanted to say how impressed I have been with the standard of your Chevallet displays. The originality and execution of the routines has been of the highest order and I'm therefore pleased to announce that you have all passed your Chevallet test. Congratulations!"

Gabrielle flung her arms around Domino in delight. "We did it," she cried.

Domino nudged her gently. "You did it, little angel. I'm very proud to be your partner."

All around them, Cherubics and chevalanges were happily congratulating each other.

Then Madame Seraph called for quiet once more. When she had everyone's attention, she said, "I am pleased to announce that all of you will be awarded the Chevalange Charm!" She paused for a moment to let the news sink in. But the best was still to come. "I am also thrilled to tell you," she continued, barely able to hold back her smile, "that this year, the charms will be presented to you by none other than the Snow Angel herself!"

A gasp ran through the assembled throng

and then the cheers rang out.

Gabrielle turned and gazed at her three friends in wonder. "Wow," she said, a little teary-eyed, "we really are going to meet the Snow Angel!"

Although Gabrielle was immensely pleased and proud of herself and excited about the Snow Angel's visit, the baby rabbit with eyes of midnight blue kept sneaking back into her thoughts.

"I wonder if Merry would mind if I took little Snowdrop back to Earth for the holidays!" she said.

"Why not ask?" Ruth suggested.

"I will, once I find out what Madame decides should happen with them," said Gabrielle.

Madame couldn't bend
the rules for Anoushka and
her family and she spoke
about the situation at tea
that evening.

"Anoushka is a lovely rabbit, but what
Merry did was breaking the school rules.
We can't allow one girl to have a pet and
not the others, so Merry knows that
Anoushka will have to live at home and
come here once in a while to visit," she
announced. "And the babies have clearly
been too much work for poor Merry. They
will need to find new homes. So, Merry and
I have agreed that any angel who would like
to take one home as a pet may do so."

Gabrielle could hardly believe there
could be so much good news in one day.

But almost as soon as the announcement was made, she began to worry. "Oh, Ruth," she said. "I must get to Snowdrop quickly. What if someone else claims her first?"

But there was already a clamour of Cherubics surrounding Merry. She'd brought the whole rabbit family along with her and had them in their hutch just outside the Ambroserie. Gabrielle saw other Cherubics claiming the little bundles of fur and she was crestfallen. Snowdrop must have been taken by someone else by now.

At last the crowds parted to reveal Merry hugging Anoushka and kissing her soft white ears.

"Ah, there you are," said Merry. "I

wondered where you'd got to."

"I'm too late, aren't I?" wailed Gabrielle. "Snowdrop's already been taken, hasn't she?"

"Of course she hasn't," laughed Merry. "There's no way I'd let anyone else take her when I know how much she means to you. It's the least I can do," said Merry. "After all you've done for me."

Gabrielle gave Merry the biggest smile. "Oh, thank you, thank you," she gasped. "I so wanted to take a part of the angel world back to Earth with me for Christmas. And what could be more perfect than little Snowdrop?"

Chapter 15

The day of the Charm-giving Ceremony arrived and Gabrielle couldn't wait to meet the Snow Angel. As she styled her hair in preparation for the ceremony, she knew that all the effort she'd put into her first term had been worthwhile.

It was Gabrielle's dearest wish to fill her charm bracelet with Angel Charms and become the best possible Guardian Angel.

Even so, she could hardly believe the day
had come at last, when she would receive
her very first charm.

The Cherubics had been given brand-
new gowns. Angel Willow had worked on
them all term, with some help from
Gabrielle and Hope. They were much more
elaborate than the Cherubics' everyday
dresses and Gabrielle was thrilled with
hers. It was made from soft pink velvet and
trimmed with swans' down. She had new
shoes too, made from the same velvet and
trim. Her halo was glowing splendidly
above her head, and she had her hair piled
up high. As she glanced at herself in the
mirror before she left Crystals, Gabrielle
thought that she really was beginning to
look like an angel.

"You deserve this," said Sylvie, from her perch on the windowsill. I'm so proud of all four Crystals Cherubics."

"Thank you, Sylvie. What would we do without you?" said Gabrielle.

As the four friends floated down the corridors to the school hall, they smelled the sweet fragrance of the white roses which spilled out from vases all around the Academy today. In the distance, the girls could also detect the mouth-watering aroma of the special Wintervale lunch.

They'd watched from the dorm window as the Snow Angel had landed in the grounds. Though they'd hardly managed to catch a proper glimpse of the legendary angel, Gabrielle had gasped at the sight of her chariot, which looked as if it was carved from ice. The magnificent white chevalange that pulled the chariot wore a bridle and headdress that seemed to be made from snowflakes.

The Angel Academy hall was garlanded with holly and spices, and each chair was bedecked with bows. Gabrielle smiled with delight when she saw that one side of the hall had been extended out into the grounds, where the chevalanges stood proudly, waiting for their young Cherubics to receive the Chevalange Charm.

"Oooh, there's Domino," said Gabrielle.

"And I see my Humphrey!" said Ruth.

Before long, the members of the school

orchestra took their places and soon beautiful angelic music drifted through the hall and out into the Academy grounds.

At last, Madame Seraph came onto the platform. "Welcome, one and all," she said. "This is a very proud day for us, and I do not want to delay proceedings by making any unnecessary speeches. So without further ado, please be upstanding for the Snow Angel!"

Gabrielle looked on in amazement as the Snow Angel flew to the platform. She was delicately pretty and even the air around her seemed somehow pure and clear. Her wings were vast and shimmering. She wore a snowdrop dress, a necklace of white tulips, and her halo was made of glistening ice crystals.

Gabrielle hung on the Snow Angel's every word as she spoke to the girls of love and friendship, harmony, heart and, above all, kindness.

"You are a true angel as you have all those qualities," whispered Ruth to Gabrielle.

"No, I am not. You are a better angel because you follow your heart and it is such a good heart," said Gabrielle.

"Well, let's face it then; we're both perfect in different ways!" joked Ruth.

Gabrielle tried not to giggle.

It was finally time for the Charm-giving.

"Cherubics, please come forward," said Madame Seraph.

Gabrielle stood in line with the other girls. She was nervous and she so hoped that nothing would go wrong. The excitement of earning the charm and meeting the Snow Angel was almost too much to bear.

Holding out her arm as the Snow Angel attached the charm to her bracelet was one of Gabrielle's proudest moments.

"I believe you are from Earth," said the beautiful angel.

"Yes, I am," said Gabrielle nervously.

"You are very lucky and, I believe, quite exceptional," said the Snow Angel. "And from what I hear from Madame Seraph, you have made a great start here. Use your gifts wisely and spread your joy. Happy Wintervale, Gabrielle," said the Snow Angel.

"Thank you," said Gabrielle, beaming proudly.

She had been awarded her first charm by the Snow Angel. It was an incredible feeling. This was the first of the Angel Charms, and Gabrielle was determined to achieve every one. It was her aim to become the greatest Guardian Angel ever – to make her parents proud, to show respect to her angel grandmother and to help all those she could.

Her first term had not always been easy, but she had learned so much. And as Angel Gabrielle floated back to her seat with her other Cherubic friends, she smiled proudly. Now that her first term was nearly over, Gabrielle was starting to feel she really was an angel, at last. But she couldn't wait to get home to Mum and Dad; she had so much to tell them. She had the perfect angel gift for them too – her little rabbit, Snowdrop, with eyes of midnight blue.

THE END

Gabrielle loves her new life at Angel Academy.
If you missed it, discover how she got there in:

Wings and Wishes

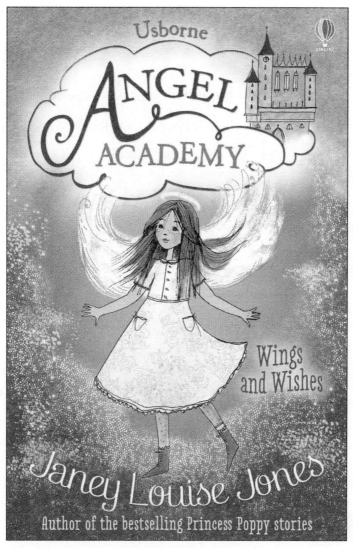

Usborne

ANGEL ACADEMY

Wings
and Wishes

Janey Louise Jones

Author of the bestselling Princess Poppy stories

ISBN 9781409538608

Look out for more magical stories in this
sparkling series coming soon!

If you enjoyed

ANGEL ACADEMY

you might also like:

Silverlake Fairy School

Unicorn Dreams

Lila longs to go to Silverlake Fairy School to learn
about wands, charms and fairy magic – but spoiled
Princess Bee Balm is set on ruining Lila's chances!
Luckily nothing can stop Lila from following
her dreams...

ISBN 9780746076804

Wands and Charms

It's Lila's first day at Silverlake Fairy School, and she's
delighted to receive her first fairy charm and her own
wand. But Lila quickly ends up breaking the school rules
when bossy Princess Bee Balm gets her into trouble.
Could Lila's school days be numbered...?

ISBN 9780746076811

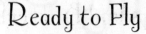

Ready to Fly

Lila and her friends love learning to fly at Silverlake Fairy School. Their lessons in the Flutter Tower are a little scary but fantastic fun. Then someone plays a trick on Lila and she's grounded. Only Princess Bee Balm would be so mean. But how can Lila prove it?

ISBN 9780746090947

Stardust Surprise

Stardust is the most magical element in the fairy world. Although the fairies are allowed to experiment with it in lessons, stardust is so powerful that they are forbidden to use it by themselves. But Princess Bee Balm will stop at nothing to boost her magic...

ISBN 9780746076828

Bugs and Butterflies

Bugs and Butterflies is the magical game played
at Silverlake Fairy School. Lila dreams of being
picked to play for her clan's team, and she's in with
a chance too, until someone starts cheating. Princess
Bee Balm is also being unusually friendly to Lila...
so what's going on?

ISBN 9780746095324

Dancing Magic

It's the end of term at Silverlake Fairy School,
and Lila and her friends are practising to put on
a spectacular show. There's a wonderful surprise
in store for Lila too – one she didn't dare
dream was possible!

ISBN 9780746095331

JOIN JAX AND BEANS AND COLLECT EVERY MAGICAL MISSION!

Moonbeans and the Dream Cafe

Jax is lonely since moving house to follow Mum's
dream of opening a cool cafe. But then a sparkly
pink lightning bolt delivers a cute alien kitten to Jax's
home, and it looks like her luck is about to change!

ISBN: 9781409526315

Moonbeans and the Shining Star

When Moonbeans announces he's on a mission to
cheer up stroppy starlet, Ruby-Rose, Jax is dismayed.
Ruby-Rose thinks she's the bee's knees because she
goes to stage school. But is it just an act?

ISBN: 9781409526322

Moonbeans and the Talent Show

Hubble, the white rabbit, is worried about his owner, Howard. He dreams of performing a dazzling magic act in the school talent show, but his act has more mishaps than magic. Can Jax and Beans help Howard shine?

ISBN: 9781409526339

Moonbeans and the Circus of Wishes

Beans has finally discovered his Earth-cat dad is living with a travelling circus – and he'll stop at nothing to find him. But Jax is worried. Could this spell the end of their adventures together?

ISBN: 9781409526346

For angels, fairies
and more sparkling stories visit:
www.usborne.com/fiction

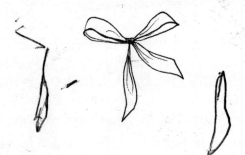